HELLO, I AM FIONA !
from Scotland

Hello, I am Fiona from Scotland!
Come inside to meet my family
and my friends...

Mark Graham
Illustrated by Mark Sofilas

www.av2books.com

Go to **www.av2books.com**,
and enter this book's
unique code.

BOOK CODE

K720323

AV² by Weigl brings you media
enhanced books that support
active learning.

First Published by

Your AV² Media Enhanced book gives you a fiction readalong
online. Log on to www.av2books.com and enter the unique
book code from page 2 to use your readalong.

AV² Readalong Navigation

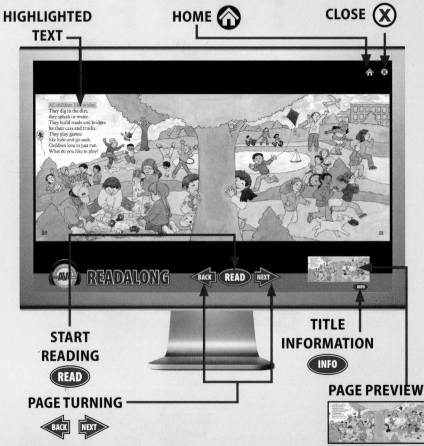

HIGHLIGHTED TEXT

HOME

CLOSE

START READING
READ

PAGE TURNING

TITLE INFORMATION
INFO

PAGE PREVIEW

Published by AV² by Weigl
350 5th Avenue, 59th Floor New York, NY 10118
Websites: www.av2books.com   www.weigl.com

ABC MELODY Éditions
26, rue Liancourt 75014
Paris, France

Printed in the United States of America in North Mankato, Minnesota
1 2 3 4 5 6 7 8 9 0 18 17 16 15 14

042014
WEP080414

Library of Congress Control Number: 2014937138

ISBN 978-1-4896-2253-2 (hardcover)
ISBN 978-1-4896-2254-9 (single user eBook)
ISBN 978-1-4896-2255-6 (multi-user eBook)

Text copyright ©2009 by ABC MELODY.
Illustrations copyright ©2009 by ABC MELODY.
Published in 2009 by ABC MELODY.

Contents

My name is Fiona. I am eight years old.
I live in a beautiful city called Edinburgh. Edinburgh is
the capital of Scotland. It has a magnificent castle on a hill.

Scottish Shortbread

BONNIE SCOTLAND

TAXI

4

a city

Scotland

a castle

a hill

From the castle, we can see the famous Forth Rail Bridge, the Scott Monument and the river. Look at the Scottish flag on the highest tower. What color is it?

Forth Rail Bridge

Scott Monument

a river

7

In Scotland, there are mountains and castles everywhere.
We have waterfalls and lochs too! "Loch" is the Scottish word for lake.
Nessie, a gentle monster lives in Loch Ness. Can you find her?

mountains

a waterfall

a loch
(a lake)

Nessie

9

I live with my mom and dad in a flat.
I have two big brothers, James and Keith.
They are twins and they love to play rugby.

a flat

twins

rugby

My mom is a tour guide. She tells tourists about beautiful Edinburgh. My dad is a train driver. He drives an old steam train to the Highlands. It's great fun!

my mom

tourists

my dad

a steam train

13

My best friend Kate has two little dogs, Mac and Bobby.
They are very cute! We love to go to Calton Hill with them.

my best friend

a dog

Calton hill

15

At my school we wear a school uniform with a tie.
My school uniform is blue and white.
Do you wear a uniform at your school?

my school

a uniform

a tie

17

At school,
we learn History,
Geography, Math, Spanish
and Scottish dancing.
I love dancing with my classmates!

Math

Scottish dancing

my classmates

On weekends, I go to Glasgow with Kate and my dad to dance in competitions. In Scotland, every family has a tartan. Boys wear a kilt in the tartan of their family. Girls wear a skirt and sometimes a sash. The colors of my family are green and blue with red lines. Do you wear a kilt?

tartan

a kilt

a sash

My family loves Scottish music!
James and Keith play the bagpipes,
my dad plays the fiddle,
my mom plays the clarsach
and I play the bodhran.

bagpipes

a fiddle
(violin)

a clarsach
(harp)

a bodhran
(hand drum)

In the summer we go up to the Highlands to stay with my granny and grandpa. They have many sheep and Highland cattle on their farm. When there is a lot of fog, Mom tells us ghost stories. It is a bit scary, but a lot of fun!

my granny
and grandpa

a sheep

Highland cattle

fog

a ghost

There are always Highland Games in the countryside with prizes for everyone. After the Games, we have a traditional meal of salmon and haggis. Haggis is made with sheep meat. Then we have a big party (a ceilidh) where everyone sings and dances.

Highland Games

a prize

salmon

haggis

a ceilidh (party)

At the end of the year we celebrate Hogmanay to welcome in the New Year. There are fireworks all over the city and everyone sings.
Happy New Year!

Hogmanay
(New Year's Eve)

fireworks

to sing

29

That's it! The visit is over!
I hope to see you soon in Scotland. Bye bye! Haste ye back!

Bye bye!

Bye!

Bye!

31